TIME

Where will they go next?

The postcard predicts
a fiery expedition!

TIME SPIES

TIME SPIES

Flames in the City
A Tale of the War of 1812

By Candice Ransom

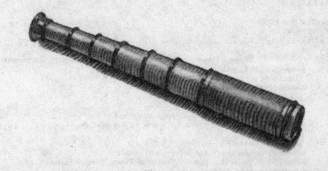

Illustrated by Greg Call

MIRRORSTONE

FLAMES IN THE CITY

©2008 Wizards of the Coast, Inc.

Cover and Interior art by Greg Call
First Printing: October 2008

9 8 7 6 5 4 3 2 1

ISBN: 978-0-7869-4973-1
620-21778740-001-EN

Library of Congress Cataloging-in-Publication Data
Ransom, Candice F., 1952-
 Flames in the city : a tale of the War of 1812 / Candice Ransom ;
illustrated by Greg Call.
    p. cm. -- (Time spies ; 10)
 "Mirrorstone."
 Summary: With the aid of their magical spyglass, Mattie, Alex, and
Sophie Chapman travel to Washington, D.C., during the War of 1812 to
help Dolley Madison.
 ISBN 978-0-7869-4973-1
 1. United States--History--War of 1812--Fiction. [1. United
States--History--War of 1812--Fiction. 2. Time travel--Fiction. 3. Magic--Fiction.
4. Brothers and sisters--Fiction. 5. Madison, Dolley,
1768-1849--Fiction. 6. Washington (D.C.)--History--Capture by the
British, 1814--Fiction.] I. Call, Greg, ill. II. Title.
 PZ7.R1743Fl 2008
 [Fic]--dc22
                                                    2008013171

U.S., CANADA,   EUROPEAN HEADQUARTERS
ASIA, PACIFIC, & LATIN AMERICA   Hasbro UK Ltd
Wizards of the Coast, Inc.   Caswell Way
P.O. Box 707Newport,   Gwent NP9 0YH
Renton, WA 98057-0707   GREAT BRITAIN
+1-800-324-6496   Please keep this address for your records

Visit our Web site at www.mirrorstonebooks.com

To Connie Harding

Contents

Danger:
Sophie Zone

"Sophie!" Mattie Chapman yelled up the stairs. "We're leaving!"

"Coming!"

Her little sister skipped down the steps wearing her mother's pink bathrobe, her father's old T-shirt that said *Oakton High School Track Team* in faded letters, fairy wings, and fuzzy elephant slippers. She carried her favorite toy, a stuffed elephant named Ellsworth.

Mattie put her hands on her hips. "What happened to the shorts and T-shirt I laid out for you?"

"Too boring," Sophie said.

A horn beeped outside.

"We have to go. Dad and Alex are waiting." Mattie closed the old oak door behind them and locked it.

Sophie hopped in the backseat with Alex. Instead of helping Sophie with her seat belt, Alex kept reading his library book. Mattie fastened the buckle.

Alex glanced over at Sophie, and then told Mattie, "Wait'll Dad sees Sophie's getup. You're going to be in big trouble."

"Maybe he won't notice." Mattie slid in the front seat beside her father. "Where are we going?" she asked him.

"To Montpelier," Mr. Chapman replied, driving onto the road. "That's the home of

James and Dolley Madison. He was one of our presidents."

"I don't suppose there are rides at Montpelier," Alex said from the backseat.

"No rides," Mr. Chapman replied. "We can't even tour the house. I'm just dropping off our new brochures in the visitors' center. But it's a nice drive and you kids haven't been out much since we moved here."

Mattie half-turned to look at Alex. Their father had no idea how many places they *had* been to, thanks to the magic spyglass.

When they arrived at Montpelier, Mr. Chapman pulled into the visitor's center parking lot.

"Wander around, but don't go far. Somebody watch Sophie." Mr. Chapman went inside the building.

Alex jumped out and ran after him.

With a sigh, Mattie took Sophie's hand.

Two women got out of a car at the same time and walked in with Mattie and Sophie. They frowned at Sophie's outfit.

"I'm a nighttime fairy," Sophie said.

"She's only five," Mattie told the women, feeling embarrassed. "My mother says she's going through a phase."

Inside, she saw Alex browsing in the gift shop. Lucky Alex. Mattie didn't think it was fair that she got stuck with Sophie. She was nine, a year older than her brother, and way more mature. Her mother said Mattie was responsible. Sometimes Mattie thought being responsible wasn't much fun.

Alex came over and said, "Let's check out that hall."

They walked through an archway and down a dim corridor lined with pictures.

"That's James Madison." Alex pointed to a painting of a red-faced man with wispy white hair. "He looks kind of grouchy."

Mattie was spellbound by a portrait of a woman with black curls. The woman wore gold necklaces and a fancy white dress. Her blue eyes seemed to gaze right at Mattie.

"Dolley Madison," she said, reading the brass plate under the painting. "James Madison's wife."

Mr. Chapman waved from the gallery entrance. "Hey kids, we have to go."

"Are you sure we don't have time to tour the house?" Mattie asked.

She had learned that old houses sometimes held surprises. Earlier that summer, the Chapman family moved from Maryland to the Gray Horse Inn in Virginia. At first, Mattie didn't like living in the old house, which her parents had turned into a bed-and-breakfast. But then in the tower room, she, Alex, and Sophie discovered the magic spyglass that took them on adventures back in time.

"Sorry." Mr. Chapman herded them out of the visitors' center. "We'll come back another time when your mother isn't at an all-day meeting."

On the way home, they drove past the large brick mansion. Mattie wondered about the president's wife, Dolley Madison. Did she wear her dresses and jewels in that house?

"Which president was James Madison?" Alex asked.

"Fourth," Mr. Chapman replied. "Right after Thomas Jefferson."

Mattie clasped her knees thinking about the secrets she and Alex and Sophie shared. They had actually *met* Thomas Jefferson. And George Washington. And a lot of other famous people thanks to the spyglass.

On the way home, Mr. Chapman stopped

at the grocery store. When Sophie climbed out of the backseat, he noticed her clothes for the first time.

"Mattie, why is your sister wearing a bathrobe in public?" he asked.

"Because I couldn't make her put on anything normal," she replied. "Mom says it's just a phase, whatever that means. Don't forget the coffee and milk."

"Thanks for reminding me. We have a full house tonight."

Mattie exchanged a quick glance with Alex and Sophie. A full house meant that one of the guests would be staying in the Jefferson Suite, the only guest room on the third floor next to the tower room. Only Travel Guides stayed in that room. And *that* meant they would be sent on a new adventure!

Back home, Mr. Chapman said, "We'll all have to pitch in to get ready. Mattie, will

7

you tidy the Keeping Room? Alex, help me with these."

Mattie watched her brother carry the lightest bag into the kitchen. All he had to do was put a loaf of bread away while *she* had to clean a whole room.

In the Keeping Room, she emptied the wastebasket and fanned the magazines on the table by the fireplace. On her way out, she stubbed her toe on a cardboard box on the floor. The box was filled with color brochures of the Gray Horse Inn and one very large black-and-white cat.

"Winchester! You're messing up our new brochures." She lifted the big cat out of the box. He glared at her, obviously annoyed.

The doorbell rang. *Maybe it's the Travel Guide*, Mattie thought excitedly. She dumped Winchester in a chair.

Before she was halfway down the hall, something small and pink shot down the stairs and yanked open the front door. Mattie nearly fainted. Sophie was greeting a guest— maybe the Travel Guide—in that ridiculous outfit!

"Hello," Sophie said to the gentlemen on the porch. "Do you have elephant slippers?"

"No, I don't," the man said. "Perhaps I could borrow yours?"

Sophie giggled. "Mine won't fit you!"

Mattie opened the door wider. "Excuse my sister. She's going through a phase."

The man laughed as he came inside. "You know, back when Thomas Jefferson was president, he sometimes met guests wearing his slippers."

"You're kidding." Mattie pictured Thomas Jefferson wearing Sophie's fuzzy elephant slippers while dragging a teddy bear by one leg.

Mr. Chapman came out of the kitchen. "Welcome to Gray Horse Inn. You're our first guest this evening."

"I'm Mr. Figley," the man said. "I believe I'm staying in the Jefferson Suite."

Yes! Mattie thought. *Let the new adventure begin!*

"Mattie, please show Mr. Figley into the Keeping Room," her father said. "I'll fix some refreshments."

In the Keeping Room, Mattie sat on the sofa, eager to speak to the new Travel Guide alone. Maybe she could get some helpful hints about traveling back in time. She and Alex often argued about bringing things from the future into the past.

Alex skidded in, carrying a pitcher. Lemonade sloshed over the sides.

"Alex!" Mattie exclaimed. First Sophie in her fairy wings and elephant slippers. And now Alex was spilling lemonade all over the place. The Travel Guide would think they were all crazy.

"I'm Alex," he said to Mr. Figley. "I hear you're staying in the Jefferson Suite. Are you going to Monticello tomorrow?"

Mattie stared at him. That wasn't the way

to talk to a new Travel Guide! Travel Guides kept their identities secret, even from them. Why didn't Alex just come right out and ask Mr. Figley where he was sending them on their next mission?

Mr. Figley didn't seem to mind. "I *am* going to Monticello. I haven't been to Thomas Jefferson's home in several years. Usually when I come to Virginia, I visit Montpelier."

"Montpelier?" Mattie said. "We were just there today!"

"Really? I'm a Madison scholar. That means I study James Madison's life. Are you children interested in Madison?"

"We just went to his house to drop off some brochures." Alex mopped the lemonade puddle with the edge of the rug.

"Montpelier looked nice," Mattie said. "But we don't know anything about Madison except that he was the fourth president and lived in that house."

"Here's something not everyone knows about Madison," Mr. Figley said. "When he was in college at Princeton, he only slept four hours a day. The rest of the time he studied."

"Wow," said Alex. "When did he eat?"

"It's hard to keep all those olden days guys straight," Mattie put in. "They all have white ponytails."

"One way you can remember them is by thinking of a symbol," said Mr. Figley. "For example, Thomas Jefferson is best known for writing the Declaration of Independence. The Declaration of Independence could be his symbol."

"I get it," said Mattie. "The Washington Monument is a symbol for George Washington."

"So what's James Madison's symbol?" asked Alex.

"The Constitution of the United States!" Mr. Figley replied grandly. "Madison is often called the Father of the Constitution. He wrote the Bill of Rights, the first ten amendments to the Constitution."

"What is the Bill of Rights?" asked Alex.

"It gives people the right to do things, like freedom of speech," said Mr. Figley.

Mattie was thinking about James Madison's wife. "Does Dolley Madison have a symbol?"

"Dolley Madison was more than James Madison's wife," said Mr. Figley. "Did you know that she helped Thomas Jefferson when *he* was president?"

"How?" asked Sophie.

"The president has many duties besides government business. He also entertains ambassadors and other heads of government."

"So you mean they throw parties?" Alex asked.

"Yes," said Mr. Figley. "But Jefferson wasn't interested in giving parties. And his wife had died years before. So Dolley Madison became Thomas Jefferson's hostess."

"I bet she told him to put on regular shoes," said Mattie.

The doorbell rang, and Mattie heard her father answer the door. More guests had arrived. Then Mrs. Chapman came into the Keeping Room.

Sophie jumped up to hug her. "Mom! You're back from the bread and breakfast meeting!"

"Yes, I am. My, what a charming outfit you have on today," said Mrs. Chapman. "It's late and you kids need to get ready for bed.

Mattie, would you help Sophie?"

"Why can't Alex?" Mattie said.

But Alex was already heading upstairs. Mattie and Sophie trudged behind him.

"I wish we could have talked to Mr. Figley longer," he said.

"Me too. I wanted to know what Dolley Madison's symbol is." Mattie was interested in Dolley Madison after seeing her portrait at Montpelier.

She stopped in front of Sophie's bedroom door. Toys, books, and clothes were thrown all over the floor. Ellsworth's house, a series of boxes Sophie had created for her favorite stuffed animal, stood in the middle of the jumble. Extreme messiness was another of Sophie's phases. Mattie would have to dig a path just to find Sophie's bed.

"Sophie," she said. "I know what *your* symbol is."

Sophie flapped her fairy wings. "I have a symbol? What is it?"

"A yellow triangle. You know, like a warning sign? And it says *Danger: Sophie Zone.*"

The Mysterious Old Book

Mattie woke up to scrabbling sounds in her closet. Someone was in there!

She sat up in bed. Sunshine slanted through her pale pink curtains. What robber would be sneaking around her room in broad daylight?

She jumped out of bed and jerked open her closet door. Sophie sat on the floor, pulling one of Mattie's lime green high-top sneakers over her small foot.

"Hi!" Sophie said. "Can I wear these shoes today?"

"No, you can't. They don't fit."

"Ple-e-e-ease! I'll stuff toilet paper in them." Sophie's bottom lip wobbled, a sure sign of a coming meltdown.

Mattie wondered how long this phase was going to last. "Soph, today is adventure day! How about we both wear purple T-shirts? We'll be like twins."

Sophie brightened. "Okay!"

Mattie got dressed too, and then went downstairs to the dining room. Sophie ran ahead, carrying Ellsworth.

Mr. Figley was sitting at one end of the table. An old green book lay on the tablecloth next to his coffee mug. Alex sat next to him.

Sliding into the chair across from Alex, Mattie said, "Sorry we're late."

Alex slapped a pancake on Mattie's plate. "Dad made your favorite today. Chocolate chip banana."

"Good morning, ladies," said Mr. Figley. "Alex was just saying how much you three love history."

"Well, we know a lot about Thomas Jefferson," Mattie said. "We've been to Monticello."

"I'm giving a lecture there today," said Mr. Figley. "I'm discussing the letters of James Madison and Thomas Jefferson. Did you know that Madison and Jefferson were best friends for fifty years, and they exchanged 1,200 letters?"

"I can barely write *one* letter to thank my grandma for my birthday present," Alex said.

Mattie poured syrup on her pancake. "What did they write about?"

"Crops, local news, politics," Mr. Figley replied. "Sometimes they wrote about things they didn't want anyone else to read, so they used a code. Both Jefferson and Madison were big fans of codes."

"So are we!" said Alex. "What kind of a code did they have?"

At that moment the rest of the guests entered the dining room. They sat at the other end of the table, chattering and laughing.

Mr. Figley lowered his voice. "Madison and Jefferson's code was based on a book that they each had a copy of. Each word was represented by three numbers."

"That's like math." Mattie wrinkled her nose. Math wasn't her favorite subject.

"How did it work?" asked Alex.

"The first number stood for the page of the book," Mr. Figley explained. "The second number stood for the line in the book. The last number stood for the position of the word in that line, counting from the left."

"Sounds complicated," Mattie said.

Mr. Figley sipped his coffee. "It isn't really. Get me something to write on and I'll show you."

Mattie fetched a postcard from the sideboard. Mr. Figley was going to need one anyway. All Travel Guides wrote a postcard that gave Mattie and Alex and Sophie a hint about where they would be sent on their next adventure.

"We'll use this as our codebook." Mr. Figley opened the old book by his plate and took a pencil from his shirt pocket. "What will our message be?"

"We like ice cream!" Sophie said.

"That's a good one," said Mr. Figley said. "You find the words you need. When

22

you write the numbers of the message, break the sentence in groups of three. That makes it harder for the enemy to figure out the code."

Mattie and the others gathered around Mr. Figley as he skimmed the book.

"Our first word is *we*," he said. "Here it is on page four, in the fifth line, and it's the second word in that line. So what would the numbers be?"

"Four-five-two," Alex said promptly.

"Correct. The code for *we* is four-five-two. So you write that down. Then you look through the book until you find the word *like*. Here it is," said Mr. Figley. He scribbled numbers on the back of the postcard.

"What if you can't find the right word in the book?" Mattie asked.

"Then you find another word or words that sound like that word," he said. "You can also use this method letter by letter. The three numbers would represent each letter in the word. The messages are longer, though."

"I still don't get it," Alex said. "Madison lived in a house out in the country. And so did Jefferson. Who cared what they wrote to each other?"

"Jefferson and Madison were both very important men. Even after we won the Revolutionary War and gained our freedom from England, not everybody agreed with everybody else."

"Weren't they glad to be away from England?" Mattie asked.

Mr. Figley gestured with his pencil. "Yes, but it's not easy starting a new country. For example, a lot of delegates from the original thirteen colonies voted against the Constitution, *including* Virginia. Our new country had a lot of growing pains in those days. One of the worst of those problems was the War of 1812."

Mattie had never heard of that war. Before she could ask about it, Mr. Figley went on. "That was why Madison and Jefferson used code. If their letters should happen to fall into the wrong hands, they didn't want other people reading what they thought."

"What about Dolley Madison?" Mattie said. "Did she write letters too?"

"Yes, she did," Mr. Figley replied. "One letter she wrote became famous. She wrote it one terrible day during the War of 1812. Because of Dolley's letter, we have an idea of what happened that day. Letters people wrote years ago give us clues about our history."

A cry went up at the other end of the table. A guest had knocked over his glass of juice. Several people began dabbing at the mess with their napkins.

Mrs. Chapman hurried in from the kitchen with a clean tablecloth. "Mattie," she said, "please clear these dishes so I can lay this down."

Mattie got up reluctantly. Why did *she* have to help? Why not Alex? Even Sophie could carry dishes.

When she returned to the dining room, she noticed Mr. Figley's place was empty.

"Where did he go?" she asked Alex.

He shook his head. "I was watching you guys and when I looked back, he was gone. Sophie, did you see him leave?"

"No, but—"

Mattie picked up the postcard Mr. Figley had left. "Oh, no! I'm not going there!"

"Where?" Alex came over.

"Cool!" said Alex. "Maybe we'll see a whole bunch of fire engines! What's the message say?"

Mattie flipped the card over. "It's just numbers. I bet it's in that same code Mr. Figley told us about!"

"Oh, it's probably just that ice cream message," Alex said.

"No. There are too many numbers," Mattie said. "It's a new message. We'd better figure it out. The message is always a clue about our mission."

Mattie wasn't eager to go on this mission. She was afraid of fire, just like she was afraid of heights and bad storms. She didn't want to go anyplace that was in flames.

"Forget it, Matt. Let's go upstairs!"

Sophie tugged on Mattie's elbow. "Look, you guys."

Something lay by Mr. Figley's plate. It was the old book, only now it was wrapped in a clear plastic pouch.

Mattie slipped the book out of the pouch and ran her fingers along the worn, dark green cover. "*New Pocket Dictionary of the French and English Language* by Thomas Nugent," she read aloud. "It was published in London in 1774!"

"That's an antique," Alex said.

"Alex, we've never had a Travel Guide

leave us anything besides a postcard. Why do you suppose he left this?"

He shrugged. "Maybe he forgot it. He was in a hurry."

"I think we're supposed to take it with us. We need it to decode the message."

But Alex had already charged to the door. "Come on!"

Mattie stuck the postcard in the book, and then put the book back in its plastic pouch. Normally, the postcards mysteriously disappeared. She hoped this one wouldn't. She had a feeling they were going to need it.

She and Sophie hurried upstairs behind Alex. On the second floor, they climbed another staircase to the third floor. Alex pushed open the bookcase-panel that led into the tower room. One by one, they crawled inside on their hands and knees.

It was Alex's job to fetch the brass spyglass from the old desk, the only piece of furniture in the room. He ran back, holding the spyglass by one end.

"Ready?" he asked.

Sophie nodded. She clutched Ellsworth in one hand and gripped the spyglass with the other.

Mattie clasped the old book to her chest so she wouldn't lose it. She took a deep breath, and then grasped the spyglass. She always hated this part.

The spyglass felt warm. Strange symbols appeared along the brass tube. The floor seemed to drop from beneath her feet. She felt herself spinning in a tunnel. Sparks of orange and red and bright yellow flickered on the inside of her eyelids.

The colors of fire.

- 3 -

The Message

Mattie's sandals hit a gritty surface. She heard people yelling and the sound of running feet. Heat seared her arms. Was it the fire that the postcard showed?

She opened her eyes . . . and froze.

A horse-drawn carriage was heading right at her! Alex, who had just appeared with Sophie, grabbed her hand and yanked her to the side of the street. The horses tore past, kicking up dust.

"That was close," Mattie said shakily. "The spyglass should be more careful where it sets us down!"

"Where are all these people running to?" Alex asked.

"The real question is, where are they running *from*. Where did we land?" She looked around.

The street was lined with houses and important-looking buildings. A group of women hurried out of a big brick house. They wore long dresses, bonnets, and lace shawls. Then Mattie saw soldiers in knee breeches and buckled shoes. The soldiers reminded her of something.

"We're back in Revolutionary War times!" she said. "Like on our first adventure!"

"Why would we go back to the same time twice?" Alex asked. "We finished that mission with George Washington."

"I know, but aren't those soldiers the same? We must be back in those days."

In the distance, thunder boomed. Mattie tipped her head back. The white sky didn't look like it was filled with storm clouds, but it was hot enough.

A wagon clattered past. Several children were huddled among the boxes and trunks piled in the back. The girls wore long dresses and aprons. The boys had on pants that buckled at the knee.

A boy stared at Mattie with big eyes.

"I think he's afraid of us," Mattie said. "Maybe we look too weird in shorts and T-shirts."

When the driver rounded the corner too fast, the children shrieked and clung to the sides of the wagon. A small trunk fell out with a bump. The trunk lid sprang open, spilling clothes in the street.

Mattie darted forward, scooping up garments. "Come on!"

They ducked behind a clump of tall bushes. Mattie sorted through the clothes.

"Girl's dresses!" she said. "I bet they fit me and Sophie. And aprons. Here's a shirt and some pants for you, Alex."

Alex frowned at the blue shirt and brown knee pants. "I'm not wearing these dumb pants."

"Yes, you are. We have to blend in."

Reluctantly, Alex put on the old-fashioned clothes. "Since you know so much, Miss Genius, what's our mission?"

"I haven't a clue," Mattie said. That was the toughest part of their trips back in time. They always had to figure out their missions on their own.

Mattie stuffed their modern clothes under the bush. Then she picked up the old book she had brought back in time.

"I told you that we need to figure out what the numbers mean on the back of the postcard. Maybe then we can find out our mission." She glared at Alex. "Thanks to me," she said importantly, "we still have the postcard."

Alex crossed his arms. "Are you saying I should have brought the postcard?"

"You don't do much of anything these days," Mattie said, opening the book.

She gasped as she stared at the first page. Alex and Sophie leaned over to see.

"Somebody wrote their initials in the book," said Alex. "T.J."

"*Thomas Jefferson*!" Mattie said. "It's *his* book! It has to be!"

"Wow! Let's decode the message quick." Alex found a scrap of paper on the ground and picked up a charred stick to write with.

Mattie turned the thin, brittle pages carefully. The type was small and hard to read. "Page one, line one, fourth word—that's *meet*."

Alex wrote down each word. When they were finished, he read the message. "M*eet me at wileys tavern gem me*."

"Huh? What's a wileys tavern gem me?" Mattie asked.

"And who exactly is supposed to go there?" Alex said. "This message doesn't make any sense."

"I guess it would to the right person," Mattie said. "Maybe it was meant for Thomas Jefferson." She slipped the dictionary in the pouch and put it in her apron pocket.

"Then why give it to us—"

The thunder grew louder. Mattie wiped her forehead with her sleeve.

"If we're going to have a storm, I wish it

would get here," she said. "At least it would cool off."

"That's not thunder," Alex said. "It's a cannon."

Mattie shivered despite the heat. "There must be a battle close by! No wonder everybody is so afraid."

An African-American man galloped down the street on a wild-eyed horse. He stood in the stirrups and waved his hat as he yelled, "Clear out! Clear out! General Armstrong has ordered a retreat!"

Men and women ran down the street screaming and wailing. The whole town was in a panic.

We need to know what's going on, Mattie thought. She swallowed, and then almost stepped in front of the charging horse.

The man jerked the horse's reins. "Missy, you could have been hurt!"

"Mister, could you please tell us what's happening?" she asked. "We—we lost our parents and we're really scared."

"The British are in Bladensburg, only four miles from here," the man said. "President Madison sent me to warn people to get out while they can."

"President Madison? Isn't this the Revolutionary War?"

"Gracious, were you hit on the head?" he said. "That was thirty-five years ago."

Just then a man in a crooked wig rushed up. "James Smith—what news?"

"The British are on their way," James Smith told the man. "The Americans can't stop the invasion. They are in full retreat."

"The capital is doomed!" The man dashed away, his wig slipping even more.

"I've got to go," James Smith said to Mattie. "You children follow everyone out of the city. Get over the bridge to Virginia. You'll be safe there." Nudging his horse, he sped off.

"What were they talking about?" Alex asked. "What capital?"

"The capital of the United States," Mattie said. "Alex, we're in Washington D.C.! And this must be the War of 1812, the war that the Travel Guide told us about."

Alex's eyes widened. "If the capital is doomed, like that guy said, then that must be our mission."

"What is?"

"To save Washington," said Alex.

Mattie felt like running away with the rest of the people fleeing the city. How could they save a whole *city*? Then she noticed that several people were hurrying from a huge mansion across the street. A wagon was parked out front.

"I wonder what's going on over there?" she asked.

"Let's check it out," said Alex. "Maybe we'll find out more about what we're supposed to do."

The cannon boomed louder, and a horse reared.

"Watch out!" Mattie said. They took a shortcut across the lawn so they wouldn't be trampled by the frightened animal.

At the mansion, men carried out boxes that they loaded into the wagon. Mattie glanced in the wagon when they went back inside. The boxes were packed with important-looking papers, books, fancy candlesticks, and a small clock.

"Looks as if somebody is moving," she said.

The two men came back with a coil of rope that they began tying around the boxes.

One said, "This wagon is full, but she won't let us go yet."

"We must get to Maryland before the roads are closed," the other man remarked. "Surely she knows that."

Who is she? Mattie wondered. Maybe someone in the house could help them with their mission.

She sidled toward the steps, signaling for Alex and Sophie to follow. They slipped inside the house. They stood in a large hall lined with lamps. Mattie heard voices coming from a room down the hall. They tiptoed into an empty dining room with a large table and more chairs than Mattie could count.

The table was set with china and silverware. At one end of the room hung a life-size painting of George Washington. Washington wore a black suit and white stockings. He held his hand out. His mouth was set in a tight line as if his shoes pinched.

Still tracking the voices, Mattie sneaked into another room that was also empty. She noticed a brass spyglass just like theirs lying on a delicate table. A quill feather pen, a bottle of ink, and a half-finished letter lay beside the spyglass. Mattie wondered if the spyglass was magical like theirs.

The voices were coming from the next room. Mattie, Alex, and Sophie edged just inside an oval-shaped room. Hiding behind a sofa, they peeked out to see floor-to-ceiling windows flooding the room with light. Heavy red velvet curtains draped the windows. A man teetered on a ladder, unhooking the drapes from the rod.

"Be careful, French John," said a woman wearing a long purple dress. Black curls

peeped out from beneath a purple turban decorated with a peacock feather. "I intend to put those curtains back when this is over."

"I am almost done," said French John. "Will you leave now?"

"Not yet. I should finish my letter to my sister." The peacock feather bobbed as the woman spoke.

She looked familiar. Then Mattie remembered where she had seen the woman.

"Alex," she whispered. "Do you know who that is? It's—"

Just then, something blue and gold swooped into the room. The creature let out an unearthly screech.

French John nearly toppled off the ladder.

Mattie opened her mouth to scream.

A Parrot and a Painting

A huge bird settled on the back of a chair. Mattie's knees felt watery with relief.

"A parrot!" Sophie said. "Oh, boy!"

Before Mattie could stop her, Sophie slithered out from behind the sofa and crawled over to the chair.

"Look at the claws on that bird!" Alex said. "And that hooked beak! Sophie may be in real trouble this time."

But the parrot cocked his head at Sophie,

and then gently nibbled a strand of her hair. Mattie blinked, amazed at the way her little sister could communicate with animals. After a moment, Sophie crawled back.

"Her name is Polly," she whispered.

Mattie was glad the people in the room were too busy to notice Sophie.

"Madam," French John said to the woman in the purple turban. "You'd better cage that bird if you intend to take it with you."

The woman smiled. "I was hoping you'd take Polly to the Tayloes' for me."

"I will be happy to take Polly to Octagon House," French John said.

"I know who she is," Mattie whispered. "She's Dolley Madison."

"President Madison's wife?" Alex whispered back. "We must be in the White House! Let's go find the president's bedroom."

"Alex! Shh! She'll hear us." Mattie gawked

at Dolley Madison's shimmery purple gown. She was so pretty that she was able to get French John to do what she wanted with her smile. *And she owns a parrot*! *How cool is that*?Mattie thought.

"I wish I knew what happened to my husband," Dolley Madison said.

"Mr. Madison went to view the troops at Bladensburg," said French John. "Now our army is in retreat."

"I've been on the roof looking through my spyglass, but I have seen no sign of the president," said Dolley. "I'm so worried."

So she's the one who owns the spyglass, Mattie thought.

An African-American teenage boy entered the room. "Mrs. Madison, what do you want me to do about dinner?"

"Bring the drinks from the cellar, please, Paul," she said. "When my husband and his men return, they will need refreshment."

People bustled in and out the room, carrying boxes. French John staggered out with the stack of folded drapes. A man in a blue coat came in, twisting his hat nervously in his hands.

"Mrs. Madison," he said. "Why are you still here?"

"My husband asked me to pack his papers, Colonel Carroll."

"The carriage is outside. I've come to take you to Bellevue. You'll simply have to leave the rest of these things behind."

Dolley looked thoughtful. "You know, this house does not belong to me. It belongs to the people of America. I don't mind leaving my clothes, but all these lovely furnishings—"

Colonel Carroll made an impatient noise. "We don't have time to pack anymore,

Mrs. Madison. The British are storming the gates!"

"British!" squawked the parrot, flapping his huge wings. "British-british-british!"

"Kindly tell that parrot to be quiet," Colonel Carroll said.

"Polly is a macaw, not a parrot." To the bird, Dolley said, "Polly, please behave. Or else French John won't take you to Octagon House."

French John returned with two men on his heels.

"The wagon has left, Mrs. Madison," he said. "Now it is your turn."

"Not yet!" Dolley whirled from the room in a swirl of purple skirts. All the men ran after her.

Mattie, Alex, and Sophie crept out from behind the sofa and sneaked into the dining room. They crouched beneath a long sideboard. Mattie wondered what Dolley was up to.

Dolley pointed to the painting of George Washington. "We must save that picture! I don't want it to fall into the hands of the British."

One of the men who had arrived with French John tapped the portrait. "The frame is bolted to the wall. It will take an army to get it down."

"Jacob Barker," Dolley said to him. "You and Mr. DePeyster will save that painting, won't you? Or else destroy it!"

Wow! Mattie thought. Dolley Madison wasn't letting those men boss her around.

Colonel Carroll wrung his hands. "Mrs. Madison, there is no *time*. You must come with me!"

"I'm not leaving until this painting is safe," she said stubbornly.

French John left and came back with the ladder. He propped it by the picture, then climbed up while the teenage boy held the ladder. The other men handed him tools.

"The frame is screwed into the wall," French John said.

Colonel Carroll and Jacob Barker leaped forward to help, but no one was able to unbolt the frame.

"Break the frame," Dolley ordered. "Paul, fetch a hatchet."

The boy scurried out, bringing back a hatchet. He swung the hatchet and smashed the heavy frame. Mattie imagined that George Washington shuddered from the blow.

"Stop!" French John said. "You may damage the painting. Let me try." With his penknife, he pried the enormous canvas from the outer frame. After several moments, he slid the painting to the floor. The picture was nailed to a smaller, lighter-looking frame.

"Thank heavens!" Dolley said. "Now we just need to get it out of the city."

"The wagon is gone," French John said.

Dolley looked at the two newcomers. "Mr. Barker . . . Mr. DePeyster?"

"We have a wagon," said Jacob Barker. "We would be happy to take General Washington's portrait to safety."

The men lifted the portrait and carried it outside.

Mattie had a sudden flash. "We have to go where the painting goes!" she whispered.

"What about our mission?" Alex asked.

"Maybe that is our mission!" Mattie said. That painting was very important. Mattie wanted to make sure it was safe. It was the least she could do for Dolley Madison.

"What's so great about an old picture?" said Alex.

"It's not just a picture," Mattie said. "It's a *symbol*. You know, like Mr. Figley talked about? That painting is a symbol of—of America!"

She peered around the side of the sofa. No one was looking in their direction. "Let's go," she said.

Keeping their heads low, Mattie, Alex, and Sophie skittered from the dining room. Mattie glanced back to see Dolley Madison scooping silver forks and spoons into a draw-string purse.

"N*ow* you must leave," Colonel Carroll was telling her. "I can't tell you how long it will remain safe enough to travel to my house. Bellevue is across town."

"I can't . . . until I know where . . . emmy . . . will meet me." Some of Dolley's words were lost in the clatter of flatware.

"We cannot delay," Colonel Carroll

insisted. "Now is the time!"

Mattie wondered who Emmy was. Dolley Madison's sister? Her best friend?

"Come on!" Alex said and tugged her down the hall.

Outside, Mattie glanced around for the men with the painting. She spied them down the street, sliding the painting into the back of a wagon. Bales of hay sat on the ground.

"We have got to go with that painting," Mattie said.

"Are you nuts?" asked Alex. "Those guys will see us."

"Wait a minute." Mattie watched as Mr. Barker and Mr. DePeyster shredded hay and covered the painting.

"They're going to smuggle the painting out of town," Alex said. "Pretty smart."

"They're going to smuggle us out too. Get ready."

When the men took the unused bales of hay to the nearby stables, Mattie jumped into the wagon. Alex hopped in beside her. They both helped Sophie up, and then quickly burrowed in the hay. Mattie heard the men return. The wagon shifted when they climbed into the seat.

"Giddyup!" called Mr. Barker.

The horse lurched down the street. The wagon swayed from side to side. Mattie lay beside the portrait of George Washington, clinging to the floorboards with her fingernails.

The wheels churned up a fine red dust that blew into the wagon. Mattie sneezed and Sophie coughed. Mattie hoped the men wouldn't hear them. The streets were filled with horses and carriages and people shouting.

Suddenly someone yelled, "Halt!"

The wagon jolted to a stop. Mattie lifted her head to see what was going on.

A stranger clutched their horse's bridle. He scowled at the men in the wagon.

"Get down," he growled.

"Unhand that animal at once or I'll—" Mr. DePeyster began.

"Or you'll what?" the man sneered. "Call the army? They're runnin' from the Redcoats. Which is what I mean to do, only I need a wagon first."

"That guy's a bandit!" Alex whispered.

Mattie was afraid that the bad guy would steal the wagon. Where would he take them and the painting?

Alex showed Mattie a rock he had found. She nodded. He poked his arm through the straw, and then let the rock fly. It landed with a plunk near the bandit.

"What's this?" the man cried.

Mr. Barker cracked his whip over the man's head and yelled, "Giddyup!"

The horse lunged ahead. Mattie and Alex ducked back under the straw. She never realized that leaving the city would be so dangerous.

The wagon rattled down the road, bumping over stones and plunging into potholes.

After what seemed like hours, they finally stopped.

Mattie peered through the wisps of hay. Instead of houses and buildings, tall trees lined one side of a narrow lane. A cornfield stretched along the other side. A neat white farmhouse stood next to a barn on top of the hill. Mr. Barker and Mr. DePeyster were striding up to the farmhouse. A man answered their knock on the front door and listened while the other men talked.

"We can't stay here," said Alex to Mattie. "They'll catch us."

Mattie, Alex, and Sophie climbed out of the wagon and hid in a clump of bushes by the lane. *Just in time*, Mattie thought.

The farmer and the two men walked over to the wagon. Brushing off the straw, they slid the painting out and carried it up to the farmhouse.

"Let's get back in the wagon," Alex said. "Quick. Hurry!"

But the front door opened again. Jacob Barker headed down the hill toward the wagon.

"Time to rest, fella," he said to the horse.

He unhitched the reins, and then lifted the horse's feet one by one to check for stones in his hooves.

"We'll be staying here tonight, so you will have a nice barn to sleep in. Be glad you aren't Jemmy's horse. Poor Liberty is caught in the middle of the British invasion." He patted the horse's neck and led him up the hill toward the barn.

Alex grabbed Mattie's arm. "What are we going to do *now*, Miss Genius? I told you this was the wrong mission! The painting's safe. And now we're stuck here in the middle of nowhere when we were supposed to be back in Washington saving the city!"

Mattie didn't answer. Mr. Barker had said *Jemmy*! Now she knew Dolley Madison wasn't waiting for her sister or a friend named Emmy. She was waiting for her husband, *Jemmy*!

And then she realized something else.

"The postcard," she said to Alex and Sophie. "I know what that the message on the postcard means!"

5

Danger on the Road

"President Madison," Mattie blurted. "He's Jemmy!"

"What?" Alex stared at her.

"I bet Jemmy is James Madison's nickname," Mattie said. "When we were leaving the White House, I thought Dolley Madison said she wouldn't leave until she heard from 'Emmy.' But now I know she said '*Jemmy*.' "

"What does that have to do with the postcard message?"

"We got the postcard message all wrong," Mattie said. "It's not *meet me at wileys tavern gem me*. It's *Meet me at wileys tavern, Jemmy*. Don't you get it? James Madison is Jemmy! This is a message from him to his wife, Dolley, telling her where to meet him!"

"So why didn't he sign the message Jemmy?" Alex asked. "Why did he write it wrong?"

Mattie explained. "The word *Jemmy* isn't in the book, so he wrote *gem me* instead."

"But why did Dolley go to that Colonel Carroll guy's house?" Alex asked. "Bellevue or whatever it was called?"

"Because she didn't know she was supposed to meet Jemmy at the tavern!" said Mattie. "We've got to go to Bellevue and deliver that message. That is our mission! I'm sure of it." Helping Dolley Madison had to be the reason they were sent here.

"You're wrong!" Alex said. "We're not supposed to go with some dumb painting. Or deliver a message. We're supposed to save Washington!"

"How do you know? You haven't done anything on this mission," she said.

"I threw a rock and scared the bandit," he said. "That's something."

Mattie pushed her hair off her sticky neck. She was tired of sitting in these itchy bushes. She was tired of being hot. And she was tired of arguing.

"All right. You're the big hero," she said.

"I just want to make sure the message really is from Madison."

Sophie spoke up. "Yes, it is."

"Are you sure?" Mattie asked her sister.

Sometimes Sophie knew things that she and Alex had no clue about. It was one of her strange habits, like the way animals instantly became her friends.

"Sophie," Alex said. "Tell us what you know."

But Sophie adjusted the bow around Ellsworth's neck and wouldn't say more.

"We have to tell Dolley Madison that her husband will meet her at Wiley's Tavern," Mattie said. "And we have to go now."

"Back to Washington? The British might be there. We could be captured as prisoners."

"They won't bother with us. We're just kids." Mattie stood up from the bushes.

"We can't walk all the way back to the city," Alex said. "It'll take forever."

Mattie lost her temper. "Stop whining! Maybe somebody will give us a ride."

They ran down the farmer's lane until they reached the main road. Carriages wheeled by, filling the air with choking dust.

"Everyone is leaving," Alex said. "Nobody is going *to* the city."

"She is." Sophie pointed to a wagon driven by a woman. Sophie added, "The horse's name is Tom."

She skipped up the road.

Alex stared at Mattie. "How does Sophie do that? The horse is a block away!"

"I don't know. Maybe this phase she's going through means she is getting stronger powers or something."

She and Alex had always wondered about the way Sophie could predict things that hadn't happened yet. But they never called it anything. She wished she hadn't said the word *powers*.

By the time the wagon reached them, Sophie was sitting beside the driver.

"This is Mrs. Lundquist," Sophie said. "She'll take us to Washington."

"Hop in back," Mrs. Lundquist told Mattie and Alex. "You're lucky I came along. Everybody else is skedaddling out of town. I'm going in to hire out Tom and my wagon. I should turn a tidy profit."

Mattie climbed in the wagon. "Do you know where Colonel Carroll's house is?"

"Bellevue? Yes, it's in Georgetown." Mrs. Lundquist clucked her tongue and Tom took off at a trot.

Leaning against the back of the jostling wagon, Alex said to Mattie, "What if Dolley Madison isn't there? Then what?"

Mattie didn't answer. She was listening to Sophie chatter to Mrs. Lundquist. Usually her little sister was shy around strangers and didn't talk much. Mattie worried that Sophie would slip and say something about their mission, or tell the woman that they were from the future.

"Look, the houses are getting closer together," Alex said. "We're coming into the city."

Mrs. Lundquist drove the wagon down a side street and stopped in front of a fancy brick house. "This is it," she said.

Mattie and Alex scrambled out of the wagon, and then helped Sophie climb down from the driver's seat.

"Bye, Tom," Sophie told the horse. "You'll be okay."

When the wagon pulled away, Mattie noticed an open carriage parked in the street. A man waited behind the team of gray horses. A woman in purple was climbing into the carriage, assisted by Colonel Carroll.

"That's Dolley!" Mattie cried. "I bet she's not staying here after all."

"Maybe she got Madison's message," said

Alex. "And she's on her way to Wiley's Tavern."

"Then why would *we* have the message on the postcard? I'm sure it's our mission to deliver it to her."

"How are we going to do that?" Alex said. "We can't just run over and tell her. She'll think we're bonkers."

"You're right," she said. "She won't believe us. We'll figure something out."

Cannons boomed closer than ever. A girl in the carriage clapped her hands over her ears. The man jumped up on the seat and slapped the horse's reins. Only Dolley Madison seemed calm as their carriage sped down the street on two wheels.

"We can't let her get out of our sight!" Alex said.

Mattie glanced down the street. Another wagon was heading their way. It worked once—it should work again.

"When I shout three," she said. "Hitch a ride!"

As the wagon rolled by, the kids sprang into the back. The wagon was piled high with boxes and bundles, but there was room for them to squeeze in. Mattie found a blanket. She pulled it over them so they could peer out, but still stay covered.

"We're following Dolley's carriage," Mattie said. "I hope we can catch up."

A group of American soldiers raced down the road. Their uniforms were coated with dirt and dust.

"The British have entered the city!" one man bellowed. "Head to Virginia! Save yourselves!"

Suddenly people began pitching trunks and mattresses out of their wagons. A couple in the carriage beside them stopped to toss chairs and a table.

"What are they doing?" Mattie asked.

"I think they're throwing stuff away so the horses can go faster," Alex said.

Wagons and carriages jostled for space on the clogged road. People shook their fists at one another. Mattie worried that they would be caught in a fight. But the driver of their wagon kept their vehicle on the edge of the road and went around the arguments.

Through the cloud of dust, Mattie spotted Dolley Madison's carriage ahead of them. The gray horses stood out among all of the black and brown horses. And Dolley's turban made her a good target.

"Keep your eyes on that purple turban," she said to the others. "If Dolley's carriage turns off the road, we'll jump out to follow."

The stifling air grew a little cooler. Mattie noticed that they were crossing a long plank bridge. Through the cracks between the planks, she saw the dark gray water rushing beneath.

"That must be the Potomac River," she said. "When we get to the other side, we'll be in Virginia."

At the end of the bridge, the back wheel of their wagon dipped into a pothole and stopped. Mattie heard the driver groan as he climbed down off the seat.

She held her breath listening to his feet crunch nearer. The driver leaned against the stuck wheel, but it wouldn't budge.

"Guess I will need my tools," the man said.

"Oh, no!" Mattie whispered, her heart sinking to her toes.

It was too late. One corner of the blanket was yanked back.

6

"Washington Is Burning!"

Mattie stared into the startled face of the red-haired driver.

"What on—? Who are *you*?" he demanded. "What are you children doing in my wagon?"

"Please don't be mad, sir," Mattie said, thinking fast. "We lost our parents. The last thing they said was to get to our aunt's house in Virginia."

"So we hitched a ride," Alex put in. "It's too far to walk."

The driver's voice became gentle. "Where does your aunt live?"

"Near Wiley's Tavern, I think," Mattie replied.

"Don't know where that is. I'm sorry, children, but I'm only going to a farm right over there. When I get my wheel fixed, that is."

"That's all right," said Alex. "We'll find our own way."

Mattie, Alex, and Sophie scrambled out of the wagon. They started jogging down the mobbed road, dodging tired soldiers, people on horseback, and baggage wagons.

Will we ever find Dolley's carriage again? Mattie wondered. She *had* to deliver that message.

Dusk draped the woods. The sounds of creaking wheels and snorting horses seemed to be muffled by the lavender shadows.

"There she is!" Sophie's keen eyes spotted

the purple turban with its bobbing peacock feather.

Dolley's carriage was turning off the road onto a lane. The kids followed, flitting from tree to tree so they wouldn't be seen. A huge white house sitting on a wide lawn came into view. The carriage pulled up to the front and stopped.

"Is this Wiley's tavern?" Alex asked. "It looks like a house."

A woman opened the door. Dolley and the young girl went inside. The driver brought their bags up the porch steps. Then he got back in the carriage and moved it around back.

"That lady left the door open," Alex said. "Let's look inside."

"Good idea."

Mattie took Sophie's hand and together they scampered across the lawn. Alex was right behind them. On the porch, they stationed themselves just outside the door. Mattie leaned in.

The long hallway was packed with women and children. Cloaks, bonnets, bags, and bundles were piled along the walls. The women's faces looked frightened. Small children clung to their mothers' skirts. Several babies were crying.

The woman who had greeted Dolley Madison at the door said to her, "I'm so glad you made it."

"Thank you, Matilda. Sukey and I have traveled a long way." Dolley sank into a chair.

"You are welcome to stay," Matilda said. "But our home is only ten miles from the city. I don't know how safe we are."

"I told you," Mattie said, as she pulled Alex and Sophie behind a huge urn. "This isn't Wiley's Tavern. It's just the house of one of Dolley's friends. We still have to tell Dolley where to meet Madison. We have to go in and give her that message."

"Are you crazy?" Alex said. "She'll think we're spies or something. There's a war going on, Mattie. Why should the president's wife trust a bunch of strangers?"

"We'll figure *something* out. Honestly!"

They slipped in the door. Mattie kept her head high, pretending she belonged there. That's when she saw a girl with long blond hair staring at them.

Alex saw her too. "Uh-oh. Caught."

The girl threaded her way through the crowd. A younger girl about Sophie's age trailed behind her.

"Hello," the blond girl said. She was a little older than Mattie, ten or eleven. "Did you have to flee your home too?"

"Um, yes," Mattie replied. "Our mother is—somewhere. My name is Mattie. This is my brother, Alex, and this is Sophie."

"I'm Pamela Martin," the girl said. "And this is my sister, Sarah."

"I couldn't bring my doll," said Sarah. "I miss her so much."

Sophie held out Ellsworth. "I'll share Ellsworth with you."

The little girls found a quiet corner and began to play. Mattie was surprised at how fast Sophie had made friends with Sarah.

"I had to leave my china tea set," Pamela said. "It came all the way from Paris, France. But Mother said we could only bring necessities."

Mattie would hate to leave behind her favorite books and her soccer trophies. She tried to cheer Pamela up. "If Sophie couldn't take Ellsworth with her, the war would be a lot worse," she joked.

Pamela's round blue eyes filled with

tears. "I don't really care about the silly old tea set. I'm worried about my father. He's a soldier and he was in that battle near Washington City. We haven't heard from Papa in days."

"I'm sorry." Mattie put her hand on Pamela's arm.

She shouldn't have made that dumb joke. This war that she had never heard of was definitely real. Little kids and even babies had to run away from their homes. And children's fathers were soldiers. That was the worst of all.

Across the hall, Mattie caught a glimpse of Dolley Madison opening the purse that sat heavily in her lap. Untying the drawstring, Dolley began pulling out the silver spoons and forks that Mattie had seen her take from the dining room table in the White House.

Dolley also pulled out a small, dark green book.

The book was an exact copy of the book in Mattie's apron pocket! *The New Pocket Dictionary of the French and English Language* by Thomas Nugent.

Mattie wondered if the other book belonged to James Madison. Dolley must have brought it from the White House. Did she know the code her husband used with Thomas Jefferson? Mattie had to find out.

"Pamela," she said. "Can you get me a piece of paper, please? And a pen?"

After Pamela left, Alex poked Mattie. "What's up?"

"Dolley has the same book as we do! I bet it's James Madison's copy. I figured out how to let her know that we aren't spies."

Pamela came back with a piece of parchment paper, a goose-feather pen, and a small pot of ink. Mattie flipped through the dictionary, dipped the pen into the ink, and then scratched some numbers on the parchment. She folded the paper and handed it to Pamela.

"Would you give that to the lady in purple over there?" Mattie asked.

"Mrs. Madison?" Pamela flashed Mattie a suspicious look, but crossed the hall to deliver the note.

"What did you write?" Alex asked.

" 'Trust us,' " Mattie replied. "Let's hope she does."

She watched tensely as Dolley Madison eyed the note, and then opened her copy of the dictionary to begin searching through the pages. After a moment, Dolley closed the book and spoke to Pamela. Pamela pointed at Mattie, Alex, and Sophie.

"Come here, child," Dolley Madison said to Mattie.

Putting on her best smile, Mattie walked over to the president's wife. Alex and Sophie followed.

At first Mattie couldn't speak. Dolley Madison was even more beautiful up close.

"Hello, Mrs. Madison," she croaked. "I'm Mattie Chapman. This is my brother, Alex, and my sister, Sophie."

"Pleased to meet you all," said Dolley Madison. "Now, what about that message you just sent. How do you know my husband's—particular method of communication?"

"It doesn't matter," Mattie said. "We need to give you another message. This one's from your husband."

"My husband, Mr. Madison?" Dolley looked sharply at them.

"Yeah, Jemmy," said Alex. "Give it to her, Mattie."

Mattie removed the scrap of paper from her copy of the dictionary and passed it to Dolley Madison.

Dolley read the note, then said, "Thank you for your trouble, children. I'm very grateful. But I'm wondering why Mr. Madison didn't send a proper messenger."

Mattie couldn't tell her that they had received the message on a postcard written in the future. "Maybe he didn't have anybody else to send it."

"Possibly. These are strange and dangerous times." Dolley stood up. "I must find Sukey and leave for Wiley's Tavern at once. I'll just say good-bye to Matilda Lee."

Mattie listened to the two women speaking in low, urgent tones.

"Matilda, I insist that you tell me,"

Dolley said. "I have a right to know."

"All right. James Monroe was here earlier," Matilda replied.

"The Secretary of War?" Dolley asked. "What was he doing here?"

"I asked him if we were safe here at Rokeby. He said we were as safe as if we were in the Allegheny Mountains—"

Dolley cut in. "*Where was Jemmy*?"

"Mr. Monroe didn't know. That's why he stopped by, to see if the president was here. I'm very sorry, Dolley. I didn't want to worry you."

Oh no! The president is missing! Mattie thought.

Suddenly someone upstairs screamed. A woman dashed to the top of the staircase, exclaiming, "Come look! Oh, it's the end of the world!"

Everyone rushed up the steps. Mattie,

Alex, and Sophie were swept along with the others. The crowd streamed into a bedroom and pressed against the windows. Mattie saw the shining black ribbon of the Potomac River. On the opposite bank, buildings blazed orange against the night sky.

"It's Washington City," a woman murmured. "It's burning!"

As Mattie stared, flames seemed to swallow the buildings. The scene was reflected in the dark mirror of the river, as if two cities were on fire. Mattie remembered the Travel Guide's postcard.

A loud explosion rocked the skyline. Sparks flew up like fireworks. Several women began to cry.

"Wow!" Alex said. "The White House is on fire! Good thing we got out."

Mattie couldn't believe her eyes. She, Alex, and Sophie had visited the Smithsonian museums and gone to the Cherry Blossom Festival there. And now the nation's capital was being destroyed.

Where Is the President?

The women came downstairs. Dolley Madison wasn't crying, but Mattie could tell she was upset.

"It's too late for Sukey and me to leave," she told Matilda. "And too dangerous. We'll stay the night."

Alex pulled Mattie aside. "Let's go home. We delivered the message. Our mission is over now."

"We can't go yet."

"Why not?" Alex said.

"President Madison is missing." She told him what she had heard. "We have to help Dolley find him."

"You're nuts!" Alex declared. "We've never stayed back in time when the mission had been completed."

"We're not staying for fun. Our mission isn't *finished*."

Alex reached into his pocket for the spyglass. "You stay. Sophie and me are going to go home."

"All right!" Mattie said. "Let's go home. But if we read in a history book that Madison was hurt or something, blame yourself!"

He put the spyglass back in his pocket. "You'd better be right, Miss Genius."

Matilda Lee clapped her hands. "Time for bed, everyone. The children will all sleep in a bedroom upstairs."

Alex shot Mattie a dark look as they followed all the other kids upstairs.

"Oh, boy!" said Sophie, when she saw the quilts and blankets on the floor. "It's a slumber party!"

Mattie tried to get comfortable on a quilt. Sophie fell asleep next to her, hugging Ellsworth. Pamela Martin's little sister, Sarah, snuggled against Mattie's back.

The room was stuffy. There wasn't even the slightest night breeze, only the smell of smoke from the burning city drifting through the open windows. Mattie sat up, feeling hot and restless. She could see the humped shape of Pamela on the other side of Sarah. Across the room, Alex dozed with the boys.

How can anyone sleep on a night like this? she wondered. What if the British army crossed the Potomac River and started burning houses in Virginia too? Worse, what if they couldn't find President Madison?

The next morning, everyone was up early. The women washed and dressed the younger children. In the big, brick-floored kitchen, Matilda Lee and her servants passed out bowls of cornmeal mush and ham-filled biscuits.

Mattie's biscuit lay untouched as she gazed out the window. Outside, smoke billowed over the trees in the distance. Washington must still be on fire.

She wondered if she had done the right thing. Maybe they should have gone home. But she had to help Dolley meet Jemmy.

Alex broke into her thoughts. "Any idea what we do next, Miss Genius?"

"Quit calling me that!" Mattie said.

Dolley Madison bustled into the kitchen, wearing the same purple gown and turban.

Mattie wondered if the First Lady had slept at all.

"Matilda," Dolley said. "Sukey and I will be going. Thank you so much for putting a roof over our heads last night."

"Where are you going?" asked Matilda.

"Wiley's Tavern. I had . . . a message that Jemmy will meet me there." Dolley flicked a glance at Mattie, Alex, and Sophie.

When Dolley left the room, Mattie slid off the bench. "Let's go," she said quietly to Alex and Sophie.

"I'm still hungry," Alex said, biting into his third biscuit.

Pamela came over with Sarah. "You're going to Wiley's Tavern too, aren't you?" she asked Mattie.

"Why do you say that?" Mattie said.

"You've been watching Mrs. Madison like a hawk ever since you came here. And you gave her that message," said Pamela. "Are you mixed up with the enemy?"

Mattie shook her head. "No, we're Americans just like you."

"I'm glad. I like you," Pamela said.

"I can't tell you what we're doing," Mattie said, "but you must be quiet."

Pamela walked with them to the door. "Be careful."

"We will." Mattie started to leave, then turned back. "I hope you get to go home soon so you can play with your tea set. But mostly I hope your father is all right."

She, Alex, and Sophie slipped out of the house in time to see Dolley's carriage turn onto the road at the end of the driveway.

"Run!" Mattie said. "Don't let them get away." She started to sprint across the lawn.

Alex tugged her apron strings. "Matt, the

carriage is going too fast. We'll never catch up to them."

Mattie gazed sadly down the driveway. Dolley Madison was gone, and Mattie couldn't help her any more. She coughed. Her throat and nose hurt from the smoke. Menacing dark clouds were gobbling the dull gray sky. More smoke? Or was it a storm? The wind picked up, tossing the treetops.

"When I grow up," Sophie said, "I'm going to have a purple hat like Dolley Madison's. With a blue feather stuck in it."

"You'll probably be president of the United States." Alex bowed. "President Sophie Chapman."

Sophie giggled. "President Sophie!"

Mattie rubbed her stinging eyes. Should she ask Sophie where James Madison was? If he was safe could they go home? But she couldn't use her little sister like a crystal ball.

Just then Mattie heard something rustling in the woods.

Mattie jumped. "What's that?"

"How should I know?" Alex said.

"What if it's a bear?"

"Then he'll probably take one look at your sour face and run." Alex picked up a rock and recklessly threw it into the woods, in the direction of the noise.

Mattie clutched his arm. "Have you lost your mind? If that's a bear, he'll chase us!"

The crashing sound grew louder.

"It's that boy," said Sophie. "Not a bear."

"What boy?" Mattie asked.

But Sophie had already started running into the forest. Mattie and Alex dashed after her.

The woods were thick with snakelike vines that tripped them. Prickly bushes snagged on Mattie's long dress and apron. But at last they came to a clearing. Sophie was already talking to a teenage boy. Mattie recognized him from the White House. He had helped take the painting of George Washington down from the wall.

The boy glanced over at Mattie and Alex. "Hello," he said. "Are you lost too?"

"No," Mattie said. "I mean, we came from a house just over there. I think it's called Rokeby."

The boy nodded. "The president tried to find Rokeby last night, but it was too dark and we got tangled up in the woods."

"Wait. Did you say the president?" asked Alex.

"Yes, I'm Paul Jennings. I work for Mr. Madison. I met him at the president's mansion yesterday, just before the British got there. We all traveled to Virginia together.

President Madison and his cabinet had a rough time of it."

"Why did the president take his furniture?" asked Sophie.

"The cabinet is the men who work for Mr. Madison," Paul explained. "That's what they are called."

"Then President Madison and Dolley Madison just missed each other!" Alex said.

"What?" Paul asked. His expression turned serious.

"Dolley—I mean, Mrs. Madison stayed at Rokeby last night, where we were. She just left for Wiley's Tavern," said Mattie. "Where *is* the president, anyway?"

"Just behind me," said Paul. "He sent me ahead to find the road."

"We can show you that." Alex pointed. "See the end of the driveway through those pine trees? The road is right there."

But Paul had turned away to look in the opposite direction. Several men on horseback straggled toward them.

Mattie stared at them. The smallest man wore a black coat and pants covered with dust. His white hair was streaked with soot. He slumped wearily in his saddle.

"Mr. Madison," Paul Jennings said, striding over to the man.

This was James Madison! Mattie couldn't believe she was looking at the fourth president, the Father of the Constitution. He looked so . . . *ordinary*.

The horse that the president was riding snorted and pawed the ground. The president held the reins loosely in the fingers of one hand. Too loosely, Mattie noticed. Then the horse reared on his hind legs, and James Madison lost his grip.

Tornado!

The president pulled the reins just in time. He remained in the saddle, but the horse danced and whinnied.

"That's not Liberty," Sophie said.

James Madison stared down at her in surprise. "No, it isn't. I had to borrow this unfamiliar and rather balky mount."

"He's afraid," Sophie said. "That's why he's so hard to ride."

"Well, that makes two of us." He smiled at

her. "You seem to know a lot about horses."

"That's because I love horses better than anything, except Ellsworth." She held up her stuffed elephant. "This is—"

"Sophie," Mattie said quickly. "The president is a busy man."

"Mr. Madison," Paul said. "These young people are claiming that Mrs. Madison was at Rokeby last night. And it's right over there."

"You mean we were within two hundred yards of a bed and a hot meal instead of stumbling around these dark woods all night?" James Madison shook his head. "Is my wife still at Rokeby?"

"No, she went to Wiley's Tavern to meet you," Alex said.

"Then she did get my message!" James Madison turned to Paul. "Is this true? Why wasn't I told?"

"I only just found out, sir. These children informed me."

The wind whipped Mattie's hair into her eyes. Pushing it back, she said, "We gave Mrs. Madison your message."

The dark clouds had blotted out the sky entirely. Mutterings of thunder deepened to dangerous rumbles. The wind whooshed through the woods, ripping leaves from the trees like confetti. The horses skittered sideways.

"We're in for a bad storm," said Paul.

"Let's head for Wiley's Tavern—" James Madison's last words were torn from his mouth as the wind whipped past them with a high, screaming sound.

Mattie looked up to see a strange, greenish light. Last summer when the Chapmans had stayed at a lake in Maryland, they had been trapped in a thunderstorm. The radio warned everyone to take cover if they saw a green light in the sky.

"Alex!" she cried. "See that sky? There's a tornado coming! We have to find cover."

"A tornado!" He gaped at her. "Where are we going to find shelter in the middle of the woods? Get real, Mattie."

"We can't stay outside!" Her teeth chattered. She was afraid of tornadoes even more than heights and fire.

"Paul, lead us to the road!" James Madison yelled over the wind. His white hair flew wildly around his face.

Before Mattie could blink, rain fell as if it had been tossed from a giant bucket. Huge cold drops splashed down. In seconds everyone was drenched. The wind grew stronger, bending trees. The ice-cold rain felt like needles as it struck.

Mattie braced herself against a tree. She

grabbed Sophie, afraid her little sister would be blown away.

"The cloud—" Alex shouted. "Where is it?"

Mattie knew that he was talking about the funnel-shaped tornado cloud. They had seen lots of TV programs where black, twisting clouds dropped from the sky.

Rubbing rain from her eyes, Mattie couldn't see a funnel cloud. That meant the tornado was on its way—unless they were so close they *couldn't* see it. She didn't want to think about that.

"The road!" The president yelled again. "Must find the road!"

Paul Jennings struggled away from the clearing. But he slipped on the wet leaves and could barely stand up. The horses neighed and pranced. James Madison tugged on his horse's reins to keep it from bolting.

Mattie couldn't see her hand in front of her face. How would they ever find the road? But the woods were too dangerous. The wind could knock a tree on top of them or they could get struck by lightning.

She remembered how Dolley Madison wouldn't leave the White House until the painting of George Washington had been smuggled out of the city. Dolley Madison, Mattie thought suddenly, was *responsible*.

And so was Mattie. She couldn't just stand there. She had to *do* something. She studied the tree that she had been leaning against. It was tall with sturdy branches. The first branch was above her head, but not too high.

"Give me a boost," she told Alex. "I have to climb this tree."

"But you hate heights," he said.

"Hurry. We don't have much time." She

was afraid she'd lose her nerve.

Alex laced his fingers together. Mattie put one foot into his hands while hanging on to the trunk of the tree.

"Ready?" He shoved her into the air.

"What on earth is that child doing?" one of the men asked.

Mattie caught the bottom branch and pulled herself up. She clung to the slick trunk. She couldn't climb this tree! Then she remembered Dolley Madison sitting calmly in the carriage while people panicked and cannons boomed around her.

Just move from branch to branch, she told herself. Don't look down. Don't look up. Her legs were rubbery, but she kept climbing. At last she was high enough to see over most of the wind-lashed trees. The road was a slick, mud-covered track just beyond the treeline. By craning her neck, she could even see the rooftop of a building. Could that be Wiley's Tavern?

She climbed back down carefully. Paul Jennings helped her down from the last branch.

"The road is just over there," she said breathlessly. "And I saw a building a little ways off. Maybe that's the tavern."

"Paul, will you go ahead?" asked James Madison. "Children, ride with us."

Mattie, Alex, and Sophie each clambered up behind one of men. With Paul in the lead, they stumbled out of the woods. The storm still raged as they struggled down the road. Rain churned the red dust into mud soup. The horses could barely pick up their hooves. Mattie huddled against the wet wool coat of the man in front of her.

After a while, Paul let out a whoop. "That's it! Wiley's Tavern!"

Mattie slid down from the horse. The tavern, which was also an inn, was a large building. Several carriages and wagons were parked along the side.

The front door banged open and a familiar figure in purple rushed out. Dolley Madison raced down the steps to meet her husband. Her face was filled with joy.

The men got off their horses. Servants hurried out to stable the animals. In the confusion, no one noticed Mattie, Alex, or Sophie.

"Time to go," Mattie said. "Our mission is *finally* finished."

Alex pulled the spyglass from his pocket. "It's soaked. I hope it still works."

He held the spyglass by one end. Sophie touched the middle, and Mattie clutched the other end. She looked at Dolley Madison one last time.

The muddy road fell from under her feet. Strange green sparkles flickered behind her eyelids. Then she landed firmly on a wooden floor. They were back in the tower room.

Mattie opened her eyes. Alex and Sophie appeared beside her, dripping all over the floor.

"The dictionary! I hope it's not ruined!" Mattie cried, taking the plastic pouch from her pocket. But when she held up the plastic pouch, it was empty.

"It's gone," Alex said, awestruck. "Did the book stay back in time?

"I guess so," Mattie said. "It belonged to Thomas Jefferson, after all. We weren't supposed to keep it, only borrow it to complete the mission."

She fetched the Travel Guide's letter from the desk.

"We'll read it in my room," she said. "After we change."

Then Mattie realized Sophie wasn't wearing a purple T-shirt but a ragged dress. Alex's blue shirt was full of holes. Mattie looked down. Her white apron had turned yellow and become threadbare. "Oh, no!" she said. "We came back in clothes from the olden days!"

"We left our regular clothes under that bush in Washington," said Alex. "We're not supposed to leave anything in the past, remember?"

Mattie knew that as well as her own name. How could she have been so irresponsible? Dolley Madison wouldn't have done anything so stupid.

"I should have been more careful," she said. "I feel terrible."

"Everybody makes mistakes, even you,"

said Alex. "Don't worry about it. This whole trip was weird. First, we took that book back and it stayed back in time. And the postcard didn't disappear."

"And now we've worn clothes from the past into the future." Mattie thought of something. "Our modern clothes probably burned in the fire. All that's left is ashes and nobody could tell that those ashes belonged to the future."

Alex pulled a handful of threads from his shirt. "What about *our* future when Mom finds out our clothes are missing?"

"We'll just say the dryer ate them," said Mattie. "The dryer is always eating socks. Still, I wonder if this means our missions will be different from now on."

The pocket fell off her apron. When it hit the floor, the fabric turned to powder.

"Our clothes are getting older by the

second," she said. "We'd better change before they fall apart completely."

Alex was already crawling through the bookcase-panel. Mattie started to follow him.

"Sophie?" she said. "Come on."

"Wait a minute." Sophie stood next to the desk.

"Soph, we need to get out of these clothes, fast." Mattie hoped Sophie wasn't still in one of her phases. "I'll let you wear my lime-green sneakers."

"Okay." Sophie opened her cupped hand over one of the drawers.

Something soft and light drifted into the drawer. It was a bright blue feather, the same color as Dolley Madison's macaw.

Mattie blinked. If the feather had come from the past, it would fall apart like their clothes.

Wouldn't it?

Dear Mattie, Alex, and Sophie:

You all did very well on your mission to the "war you never heard of." Since you are curious, I'll tell you a little about the War of 1812.

Britain had been at war with France since 1793. Britain tried to keep the United States from trading with France. The British Royal Navy needed sailors. British men boarded U.S. ships and forced American sailors to work on the British ships. "Free trade and sailor's rights" became America's motto.

The United States declared war on Great Britain on June 1, 1812. The war was fought on our land and in our ports. Many battles were lost to the British. The Battle of Bladensburg led to the burning of Washington on August 24, 1814.

James and Dolley Madison were among the citizens who fled the city. We know a lot about what happened that day because of the letter Dolley Madison wrote to her sister Lucy.

The Declaration of Independence, many treaties, and other priceless documents were safely hidden in an empty house in Leesburg, Virginia.

The Americans stood their ground when the British bombed Fort McHenry in the Baltimore harbor on September 13, 1814. Francis Scott Key saw the American flag still flying that night. He wrote a poem that later became our national anthem, "The Star-Spangled Banner." The war ended peacefully with the Treaty of Ghent, signed in December 1814.

Dolley and James Madison returned

to Washington a few days after British troops had moved on. The Capitol building, Library of Congress, the Treasury, navy yard, and the White House were charred ruins. Congress considered moving the nation's capital to another city, such as Philadelphia, but instead decided to rebuild.

Work on the new Capitol began in 1815 and was finished in 1864. The exterior of the Library of Congress survived, but all the books were destroyed. Thomas Jefferson sold his private library to restock the Library of Congress. Because the White House walls remained after the fire, the reconstruction was finished in 1817.

Jacob Barker returned the picture of George Washington from the farm two weeks after the burning of Washington. The full-length portrait had been painted by Gilbert Stuart in 1796. Stuart painted Washington's face from life, but used a "stand-in" to complete the figure. A wax cast of Stuart's own hands served as a model for Washington's hands. The painting now hangs in the National Portrait Gallery of the Smithsonian, in Washington, D.C.

When James Monroe became the fifth president, the Madisons left Washington to live at Montpelier, their home in Virginia. James Madison died in 1836. Dolley moved back to Washington a year later. She had little money, but attended parties in her old-fashioned dresses and turbans.

By 1844, she had known all twelve presidents. She was the only citizen ever awarded an honorary seat in the House of Representatives. Matthew Brady, who would later become a famous Civil War photographer, took her picture. Dolley was present at the ceremony where the cornerstone for the Washington Monument was laid.

Dolley Madison died on July 12, 1849, at the age of 81. She was honored with a state funeral, the largest ever held in Washington. Dolley Madison's symbol is the act of saving the portrait of George Washington. She is considered the most loved First Lady ever.

On your next trip, Time Spies, you will return to a place you've been before.

Yours in Time,
Mr. Figley

TIME SPIES MISSION NO. 10
TWO-BOOK CODE

During the Revolutionary War and in the early years of our nation's history, patriots often used codes to send secret messages. Both Thomas Jefferson and James Madison worried that others might read their private letters. Jefferson was especially interested in codes and languages.

You and a friend can send coded messages using Jefferson and Madison's two-book code. If your message falls into the wrong hands, all anyone will see is a row of mysterious numbers!

WHAT YOU NEED:

Two copies of this book. (One is yours;
the other belongs to your friend)
Paper
Pencil

WHAT YOU DO:

Look through your copy of the book. Find a word that matches the first word in your message.

Write down the page number. That is the first number.

Then count the lines, starting from the top, until you reach the line your word is in. That's the second number.

Next, count the words in that line, starting from the left, until you reach the word. That's the third number.

Continue this process with each word, separating the numbers with dashes. Break the sentence in groups of three. That makes it harder for an enemy to figure out the code.

TRY THIS EXAMPLE:

Watch out for guy in brown

$\underline{-\ -}$ $\underline{-\ -}$ $\underline{-\ -}$
watch   out   for

$\underline{-\ -}$ $\underline{-\ -}$ $\underline{-\ -}$
guy   in   brown

Now decode this message:

$\underline{10\text{-}7\text{-}5}$ $\underline{10\text{-}7\text{-}6}$ $\underline{17\text{-}2\text{-}3}$

$\underline{59\text{-}1\text{-}5}$ $\underline{112\text{-}13\text{-}3}$ $\underline{66\text{-}12\text{-}4}$

$\underline{4\text{-}1\text{-}11}$ $\underline{76\text{-}4\text{-}2}$

Now try making up some coded messages of your own!

Read the whole series!

"What's wrong with being a chicken?"

Fowl Language
June 2008

Fine Feathered Four Eyes
June 2008

Poultry in Motion
September 2008

For more information visit:
Supernaturalrubberchicken.com